# Manipulative Minds

Eunice Oweifaware

authorHOUSE®

*AuthorHouse*™
*1663 Liberty Drive*
*Bloomington, IN 47403*
*www.authorhouse.com*
*Phone: 1-800-839-8640*

*Published by AuthorHouse    08/30/2012*

*ISBN: 978-1-4490-7271-1 (sc)*

# Manipulative Minds

written by Eunice Oweifaware

# Chapter 1

The time is 6am, the alarm clock was ringing and Yvonne woke up with a start, she refuse to get up, as she wanted to sleep more, she was not used to waking up early but she had to as it was her first day at work and she had to get there on time.

She refuse to take the job because it was not what she was looking for and it was a low paid job, but her mother and sister persuaded her to take it as half bread is better than nothing they both emphasised.

She could go on welfare and get her house rent paid, and some money given to her to buy food and pay her bills, but she realised she will just be another statistic with no future, and moreover she was fed up of being on welfare as she managed everyday of her life from when she was seventeen.

All through her degree course, she had been on welfare and grant, she thought she had finished her degree now and was a graduate so it was now time to give back to the system by getting a job as welfare could be so degrading as well as you are always seen as a scrounger and no hoper when you go for your giro.

She had honours in her bachelor degree result and was a graduate with a lot to offer as a career woman, built trying to break the glass ceiling and get a graduate job was a lot of hassle and challenge, she was finding it hard to cope with.

Graduate jobs were becoming more and more difficult, that she had to make do with whatever she had at the moment, she knew it was a false career move but she wanted to resume to look attractive,

Before Yvonne came she did not have respect for anybody because she had been in the department for twenty years, she was walking all over the staff bullying them, they were taking all the crap for the sake of keeping their jobs and putting food on their table as jobs were getting difficult to get

But as soon as Yvonne came she felt threatened because most of her staff did not go to college, and working as administrative assistants were the best thing to happen to them, so Yvonne was a big threat to her ego and her job.

Right now she was suppose to be feeling all happy and contented as she had the job and her life was going so well,she had paid her bills and she could get new clothes and buy bits and pieces of furniture and decorations to finish and decorate her flat, but the big deal is that she was becoming disillusioned with her work as she was not getting anywhere, she felt like she was stuck in one place with no future or hope and she was dreading getting up so early to go to work as she felt like she was wasting time and should be up there doing something fantastic like being the director of her own company, the more she thought about it the more she liked the idea, she thought about borrowing money from the bank, and went along to talk to the bank manager about it but after going through her credit he declared she was not fit to get, she was very disappointed about all that has happened to her but she will not give up she said, she will find a way to sort finance out she thought.

# Chapter 2

Not now Phillip said, i will have to talk you about it tomorrow, i thought you were on the pills he demanded angrily, i don't need this not right now he said i am not ready to settle down and take care of a baby, i hope you get it loud and clear he banged down the phone.

He swore at her and put down the phone, he tossed the towel he was holding down on his bed feeling very angry with Cassandra because she forgot to tale the pill and got pregnant.

Cassandra on the other hand felt embarrassed with a great remorse that he was taking it all wrong, no matter what he was suppose to talk to her and not bang the phone on her, he had been so sweet to her, and she thought the news was going to make him happy, she felt at home with him she thought she was in a better place now with him, he had disappointed her and she knew it will be the end of the relationship, as she preffered a man that would respect her and treat her well, no matter the circumstances she found herself, not just shove it in his face like he was some scub bag he picked up in the street.

She thought their union was forever, she did not know it will not last, she booked an appointment with her doctor to have an abortion as she thought she was not going to be a single parent while bringing up the child as it will be too much of a responsibility for her, she knew she was not capable of motherhood now, maybe when she is really matured then she can bring up a child, but now she will be an unfit mother she thought.

Her appointment was fixed for Thursday evening and she was looking forward to go and get it done, and forget about the relationship as it was hurting her really bad just thinking about it, she knew she had to get it done quickly and not have too much of a guilty conscience and later decide to change her mind and not have the abortion and keep her baby.

She waited till Thursday evening thinking maybe Phillip will change his mind and come and see he, but she not see him, she decided to move on and forgot about him.

Cassandra went to get the termination done in two hours and was in terrible pains and she was admitted into hospital for two days, she slept for the whole day, could not eat anything and was bleeding heavily, she felt excruciating pains and could not walk upright as she left to go home on the third day, she got a message from her mum and Natasha who was touring in East Asia.

Cassandra would normally be cheered up with Natasha going on about all this stories, but she was in a bad mood today and it did not cheer her up, she was feeling sad as life was not going her way at the moment.

She thought at twenty six she would have a serious boyfriend by now but no it was not working out, she thought this time last year she was going to celebrate christmas with a boyfriend that she adores as it was part of her set goals.

She met Phillip and things were going so well, so she thought it was going to work out and she was going to be with him forever, it was barely two months before her whole life had exploded in her face and everything was looking very bleak to her at the moment.

She wanted that perfect family, a home with a picket fence and children running around the big home but it looks like it will not happen.

Phillip was wondering what happened to her, he thought the stupid bitch was trying to trap him, he will not be roped into this kind of trap he thought, he was too smart for this.

He was sitting at the bar now and was watching the place packed with a lot of people coming in to have a drink and party, he was searching the faces of the ladies, the single ones, he did two things when he was out partying, he looked at their faces intently and their clothes, he hated untidy women so he often take his time to check them out properly, their hair skin and teeth, he was very particular about that, if she smiled with a good teeth and was tidy then he was interested, if not he keeps his distance with him and the woman, and she will be wondering if she had upset him

When he met Cassandra she had all the qualities he wanted in a woman, she was a beauty with brains and was very neat, not clingy and very independent, she strike him like a lone ranger who was not waiting to be rescued, he did not feel suffocated at all.

Two months down the line she did exactly what he did not like, he promised himself he was not going to be intimate with her again, and the affair was over, he even promised not to call her again.

He was a guy always on the move for new baits and adventure, he was guy with a big appetite for women, he was time bomb waiting to explode but he was not aware about that at all, Cassandra should be happy she left him but she was missing him like crazy and still wants him back just after two weeks from the hospital.

# Chapter 3

Natasha was having the time of her life singing those ballads with the crowd going wild with some singing along with her, and the rest of the lovers holding tight unto each other, and dancing slow to the soul music that was charging the air and blasting away so loud.

She loved it when she see the audience participating and enjoying themselves, it gives her so much pleasure to see them receiving her music so well in Asia, she will tour all of Asia before she returns to England, it is a hectic year for her but she is enjoying every day and giving thanks to God that her career is going so well, she even won a Grammy for a newcomers category, it was a surprise for her as she was not hoping to get it at all, the Grammy she won is helping her a lot as ticket sales has plummeted, she had a good manager who was advising her well and was always doing good public relation and giving her all the recognition that she needed.

She and her band members were having a good time, they disguised themselves by dressing down,

No makeup, no bodyguard and just went shopping on their own and it was the best scheme yet

No one recognised them and there was no commotion for authograph seekers, they had a wonderful afternoon and returned to their hotel to have a nice nap as they had a concert that night.

She was thinking of what she will do to give back to the community , once she gets back to England, they have helped her so much in supporting her career which was a surprise to her how it took off as she did not plan all this, Though she get on well with her band members Thelma, Rebecca and Desiree she feels really grounded with them as they are all buddies and they don't treat her as a star.

Natasha and Cassandra go back a long way, they were friends and roommates in high school and university, they both majored in psychology, and both did very well in the course, they had second class honours and were planning ton start their masters program before Natasha break into the music scene, and there was no looking back for her.

Natasha used to sing in her leisure period in the church choir when one of the sisters in church told her about this audition that was coming up in convent garden and she begged her to accompany her to the audition as she felt very nervous going by herself.

They got there, there was thousands of people queuing and when it got to Rebecca's turn she had her audition and it did not go well, Natasha was standing in the corner of the room and the man said to her pointing to Natasha, what about you darling why don't you sing for us.

 Natasha seized that two minutes opportunity, she took the microphone and sang, she gave it her all and sang beautifully she won over everybody in the room and the rest they say is history, she persuaded the producers to allow Rebecca to be one of the backing vocals and they agreed.

The music director was so excited about her that he hugged and kissed her on the cheek, he knew he found a winner, she went the next day to sign the contracts and champagne was flowing with caviar,

She and Rebecca was drunk as they drank like a fish, she knew right there that the world was their oysters, she knew it was the end of her Masters degree but she was looking forward to the rest of her life.

The car phone was ringing when Douglas driving in his Porshe reached for it and in his cracked sexy deep voice said hello and was discussing business on the phone, he studied business and accounting and was an accounts executive in Blake and Blake accounting firm in London, he had just won this contract with a major investment finance company worth millions of pound, and so far the deal is going so well that all the major players in the corporate world was calling to work with him because he has got the midas touch.

His phone had not stopped ringing since he got the contract even foreign investors are calling to work with Douglas, they had done very well in the business world, things had taken a dramatic turn as the business took a nose dive a year ago and nobody wanted to touch them or have any dealing with them, they were owing so much money as he almost declared bankrupt because of a bad deal they made that did not make profit, but they say persistent pays off, the patient dog eats the fattest bone, Douglas and his partner had to put in twelve hours shift themselves and worked very hard so they could get new customers and it payed off big time.

Douglas was born poor in saint Louis, his parents had always stressed good education to his kids, he had come home from school sometimes with no food on the table, his parents had taken two or three jobs at times to see that they put food on the table for them and also enough to pay for their school fees.

They had to work very hard for all of their children to put them through school as they were not educated themselves making it difficult for them to get that dream job that would have helped them to earn more money.

Both of his parents were minimum wage employees, as a result of that they had to work twice as hard to be able to take care of their kids, after he left university he promised himself he will work hard to get somewhere in life, his determination is paying off now.

# Chapter 4

Phillip was having the time of his life with Annabel, she was enjoying herself as he was very adventurous in bed and he was making her to moan, she had wanted him for a long time as she was very drawn to him, she had heard so many stories about him and was drawn to the bad boy status ,

he was a stud and a son of a bitch who was ready to screw anything in skirts, she was ten years older than him, she liked them young as she tends to be wary about the older guy now, she was married all her life to Isaac and had two kids by him and when they divorced she was bored and wanted to enjoy herself with no strings attached to her life, she was not looking to fall in love with anybody but have fun, she had worked very hard in life and has made money as an interior designer, she decided she was not going to sit around and let any man work all over her as a result she was going to get her priorities right.

Annabel had been hurt by Isaac several times, before he took off to live with one of his girlfriends, he was cheating on her with. She decided to kick his butt out of her life, as she had enough, he had taken advantage of her for a long time, and she decided to take him to the cleaners and got half of his wealth as he was pretty wealthy himself.

With two houses one abroad and one in England she thought it was a good divorce and now it was time for her to get on with her life, Phillips was sleeping with her friend but they broke up and she was getting married to somebody else, they became friends once he left her friend, they met again in a party one summers night in the club in the west end, he was dancing with a lady in a tight embrace as they were like practicing making love on the dance floor, they drew so much attention to each other.

Annabel started talking about him to Sarah, and was shocked to know that her friend had already slept with him and told her she had nothing to lose by sleeping with him, Sarah told her he was the best stud she had ever had but she should forget about marrying him.

Annabel started flirting with him that night shamelessly in front of his girlfriend as she was determined to sleep with him, she wanted him like she had never wanted anybody in her whole life, he was not keen to sleep with her as he was interested in the lady he was dancing with that night

He just met the lady and was dying to get laid and he decided to save Annabel for a later date, he collected her number and told her he was flattered with her, she was angry at his behaviour, he calmed her down and promised he will see her another time.

He smiled and his drop dead gorgeous smiled did the trick and she promised to give him another chance, they met up the next day and made love it was the most frenzied passionate love she had ever indulged in he was insatiable, strong and was very considerate, he was never tired, he went on and on that she thought she was going to explode in orbit.

Grace the girl she saw with him the previous night was building castles in the air, because he was so good in bed she thought she was going to marry him, Phillip was a good lover elusive and lousy in relationships, he was in love with himself, he liked Grace but he thought she was one encounters out of many, they went on several dates with Grace paying for all of the dates, she started to realise that he was a miser who was no good and was good for only one thing shag, because she not earning enough money as she works only part time and was in university, she decided to dump him because they were always arguing about money now.

Annabel was floating on cloud nine, she thought Isaac was good in bed but Phillips was the best, he knew how to please a woman, she was a satisfied customer she loved everything he did to her and she wanted to keep it that way, she started to shower him with presents, but what she did not envisaged about Phillips was that he was one selfish son of her bitch that would milk her dry.

Phillip mentioned to Annabel that he would like to go on holiday to the Carribean as he had never been there, she bought the tickets, put her business on hold and bought first class tickets with a

One week stay in St Lucia as well, she paid for hotel bills as well, it does not bother her because she had the money, she thought it was going to be a perfect holiday as they will make love all day and night.

The trip was set for a Monday afternoon, they boarded at Heathrow airport , the trip to the airport was full of kisses and touches, it was all lovey dovey with Annabel, they killed time at the airport buying and drinking beer while they talked animatedly, they nearly missed their flight.

The air stewardess had already closed the the exit door by the time they made their way to the aircraft, they knocked on the door she opened it, asked for their tickets and the boarding pass, gave

It back to them and checked them in fast so as not to disturb the pilot who was ready to fly.

They looked at each other as they sit down in business class, they were served wine and refreshments as they settle down to enjoy their business class, they knew it will be an interesting journey.

# Chapter 5

Yvonne made sure she got the date with Ralph before she left the casino, she put on her best charm and soon wooed him over, even before she left the casino he was all over her, but she did not want to be a cheap tart, as that would be just what he think he had got, she had him twisted around her little finger now, all she had to do was play hard to get and she knew he will be hers for good.

She made feel all important by concentrating on him and making out like she is really keen on him and wanted to get to know him, he willing and obliged, he gave her all the facts that that she wanted to know, he was really loaded, a tycoon businessman who owns an oil company, he is divorced and a father of three grown up kids.

He is addicted to young ladies, he will kill for a date with young ladies, who tall slim and beautiful, he would go on a date in any continent you want to dine in as far as the lady is willing to come for the ride, he could not wait to get Yvonne into bed, he thought she was willing, but what he did not know was that she was a tough cookie, he will regret meeting.

They met for lunch in a posh , swanky setting in the middle of an exclusive private club in Sloane square, he arranged for a room as well, when they finished eating, he asked her if she would like to come upstairs to a room he booked upstairs, she turned his offer down and he was surprised at her because he thought she was willing to get him into bed, she rather started to talk about herself, she told him everything she knew he will like to hear .

He was bowled over, he thought not only was she beautiful, she was very intelligent and classy as well, he asked if she would like to come work for him, she turned him down again and said no thank you, she said she was desperate to start her own business and was lacking capital to start it, he could be her business partner if he was willing to invest in the company she said.

He liked her a lot, he was fifty five years old and had been with a lot of women in his time, but what he felt for Yvonne now scared him, because he was surprised at himself, he thought love at first sight was fairy tales and never happens, but he knew it was happening now and he could not stop it, his mouth was dry, the palm of his hand was sweaty, he felt his heart racing, he wants to just grab Yvonne and kiss her and tell her how much he loved her, he had never felt like this before, not even with the mother of his children, it was really strange, he knew he wants to be with her for the rest of his life so he thought he will take his time as she was one tough cookie, he will not say anything to her but work his affection through this business by setting it up for her then he will work his magic to her heart.

She could not believe her eyes when he asked her how much she wanted for the business, to set up the business, she jokingly said a quarter of a million and he said done, with a twenty percent investment.

She asked him if he was serious about what he just said, he was laughing his head off, as for the first time he got a reaction from her with wide eyes and she was holding him in awe, which pleased him a lot, as she had always been cool and calculated, she grabbed him and gave him a big kiss when she realised he was not joking, she joked that she might as well offer herself in a platter and she caught him off guard with that joke and he was laughing so hard as she already demonstrated before that she was not a cheap tart.

She knew if she played her cards right she will be okay and this was just the beginning, Yvonne left that day with lots of anticipation about the future, it was bleak before she met Ralph that evening suddenly there was a light at the end of the tunnel for her.

She was full by the time she got home, as they had a sumptuous dinner fit for a king and a queen, she went straight to bed, she felt dizzy with happiness and could not wait for the next day to arrive, as she will be collecting the cheque from Ralph and also look for an office where she would work from, it is still a shock to her because here she was trying to sort her life out.

And out of the blue came this nice guy in shining armour to rescue her, she believed now that miracles miracles do happen, she dozed off thinking about all the things she will do the next day as it was sure going to be a very busy day.

She forgot to set the alarm clock as she woke up late, she rushed to the bathroom, had a quick shower brushed her teeth, had breakfast when the phone rang. It was her mother who was sick and wanted Yvonne to pick up some grocery for her from the supermarket, Yvonne promised to do it in the evening as it was a very busy day for her.

Her mum said she will like some fruit straight away, Yvonne said she could not manage that as she knew what she was going to do, it was no use arguing with her mum as she will not back down so she said yes knowing it will be the end of the day before she will get it.

Yvonne quickly went to Ralph's office to collect the cheque, paid it into her account then she bought the fruits and did the whole shopping and drop nit off at her mum's telling her she could not stay, she was rushing she took the day off from the office and went back home to use the internet, she got some offices and booked to see them that afternoon.

She was impressed with one of them and paid for the office as she had enough on her account to do that, she then started to work on her business plan to get it across to Ralph who was still going to look at it.

Her mum rang her again to ask what she was up to, about her not going to work today, and still cannot find time to spend with her especially when she knew she was sick and could not do a lot of things for herself today.

Mom i am sorry you are thinking that way, things are not like it seems you will know what i am trying to do soon i will let you know when I am ready, I hope you are not leaving your job, remember you have bills to pay and you need to put food on the table she empahasised.

She thought she will drop by for thirty minutes otherwise the talk will not stop, she finished with her business plan and drop it off to Ralph, they had dinner but she did not stay for too long before rushing back to see her mum who asked her to stay over and she said no and left.

# Chapter 6

Rebecca was feeling down and felt like somebody had cheated her and stole from her, she started to feel irritated and very angry as she thought about it over and over again, she felt like fate had dealt her a terrible blow and she was second best and was not earning enough.

She was the one who pulled the show together, she was earning peanuts compared to what Natasha was earning, and she was also getting all the attention in every city that they went to, she was playing second fiddle to the real star, the fans always gather around her and pushed them aside like they did not exist.

Rebecca felt that Natasha owe it to her to increase her earnings because she had been on same salary since they started and Natasha was earning three times what she was earning, she was suppose to be given special treatment from the other girls because she made it all happen, but fame had gone into her head that she had forgotten about her and all she think was herself and her stupid band, she was behaving like the world was on her feet and she could do whatever she felt like doing now.

Rebecca's attitude to Natasha's nowadays is of disgust and hatred because the genuine friendship they used to share was all gone, and all she could see was superficial acts and she felt like murdering her so that all this could will end.

Rebecca was pretending all this past year that everything was fine, while all the time she could not stand the sight of Natasha, the worst part of it was that she was always confiding in her as she believe they were cool with one another , she even disclosed how much she made the past year.

The more she talked about her success the more she hated her, she felt like leaving the band but was not ready to set her own band up, she knew her voice was not that strong like Natasha and it will be very difficult to get signed up so half bread was better than nothing she thought.

Her rage was building now to the point of explosion, she tried to kill her mum at the age of twelve when her mum will not listen to her when she tried to talk to her, she was always busy taking care of herself and going out with different men, she asked Rebecca to make her tea, Rebecca made the tea and put all of her mum prescription pills in the tea , her mum took it and went to sleep, she was unconscious when a neighbour came round to see them and found her mum, she later called an

Ambulance, she was taken to the hospital where the mum survived and could not believe her eyes that her daughter tried to kill her, she did not press charges but told the authorities she does not want to live with her again in case she tries to kill her again.

Rebecca was taken and put in a home and was later adopted by a Christian family and they made her go to see a psychiatrist, and was always going to church, she thought she was okay now, all the bent up anger was starting to surface again as she was thinking about how Natasha was treating her now.

Natasha was experiencing an attitude she had never seen in Rebecca and she was getting very worried about her beause she was very absent minded and was not paying attention when she talks to her, she wondered what was going on with her, she asked her after waiting for a long time to see if she will tell her what was bothering her but she said it everything was fine its just that she was stressed and after some good rest she will be okay.

Natasha told her if she ever wanted to talk to her about anything she was there for her, Rebecca said thanks and left, Natasha thought they had worked hard this past year and they deserved holiday to relax and take their mind of the stress they had been carrying around all year, she explained to the girls that they will not go as a group, she will rather spend time with Rebecca as she was one of her best friend, she thought the stress was driving them apart as she had barely said a word all day she told Rebecca that she wants her best friend back, the girls were very supportive and agreed that she should go with her on holiday and they could go together another time.

When Natasha surprised her with a ticket, she was not at all surprised or interested about the whole idea she told Natasha she should have asked her before buying the tickets as she had other plans and she will not be able to go with her.

When Rebecca said that she will not go with them, she decided to call the girls back again and explain what was going on and if they will be interested in going with her as she really will like to have a holiday she told them.

# Chapter 7

Yvonne had this big smile on her face as the meeting with Ralph had gone very well, she got her cheque for a quarter of a million pounds and they both signed the papers with an agreement from Yvonne on how she wanted to spread the instalments to pay back the money, Yvonne was shocked at Ralph's generosity because, here was a guy she had not slept with and he had only known her for two weeks yet he was giving her the opportunity of a lifetime, he even introduced her to his accountant to take care of her account till when she was ready to hire her own staff, she knew God was on her side as she had suffered enough she thought.

She knew a quarter of a million was a pin in the drop of an ocean for Ralph as he was filty rich, to her it meant a lot as it was the beginning of her life, she promised herself she not mess things up for herself, she will work very hard to achieve this dream of a lifetime she thought, her mark was in Publishing, she had already set up plans to publish her own fashion magazine and also publish books for unknown authors, she will later diversify into fashion, and music, as soon as she gets established she intends to employ producers to carry on the side of music producing when she sets up the production company alongside her publishing company.

She got sophisticated equipments for the music side of the business and expensive computers, and printers for the publishing side of the magazine, she hired a big warehouse where she had already divided into different sections, offices, boardrooms, music room, lab room, Printing room, the offices was well

Organised elegant with experienced editors and music producers, photographers, videomen working together as team members. The magazine was launched in three months of them being in business, they were handling all subject sex, drugs, contraceptives, relationships, fashion true life stories.

Her magazine was now ranked with the likes of vogue Elle magazines and ok magazines, she was fast becoming a household name herself, it was selling very well in Europe and America, England loved it and magazines was flying off the shelves.

Yvonne made astonishing turnover after calculating expenses and the loan, she was now ready to go into publishing, she advertised and manuscripts started flying in, she kept the editors and printers very busy that they were putting in twelve hours every day to make sure every book was published according to schedule, one of the first writers to be published was Rebecca.

Yvonne was putting in more hours than she had ever put in any job before, she was contented becuse it was her own business and she wants it to succeed, her social life was suffering but she put it on hold at the moment, she and her editors worked very hard on their first ten books and sooner than later the books were in the library in their office and was bookshop shelves across the country and abroad as well, they knew it was not their opinion that sells a book but the public will decide what they want to read, but they gave all of the books their best shot and left it for the public to decide if it was a good read or not.

Ralph was very patient with Yvonne because he know what it takes to have a successful business as he had been there before, he knew she had the tiger in her eyes when he loaned her that money, he knew she was hungry for fame and fortune, like he was twenty five years ago, he knew he will not fail when he started the business that was how hungry he was, and he succeeded against all odds.

Ralph was more impressed with Yvonne when she paid off the loan in six months, she realised she had hit a pot of gold with all the ventures she had stepped into, the three ventures was all making her so much money that she did not know what to do with money this days, Ralph knew she was going to go into other business as well, he knew she was really smart and was going to go to other countries to set up branches, and he was right, sooner than he expected she told him she will be expanding and going abroad as well, he told her he was hundred percent behind her supporting her.

Ralph was more deeply love with her now, not only was she beautiful she an edge above other women, he knew she was one smart cookie and he was not going to pay her too much attention as she will become bored and start looking elsewhere, he sends her flowers once a month which she appreciates so much as the whole office will look like a flower shop.

He invited her for dinner after six months of silence and just sending flowers once a month to let her settle down properly into her business routine, she was over the moon, she knew Ralph was playing hard to get, and it was beginning to work for Ralph, she was the impatient one that could not wait to sleep with him, he was laughing and was very happy with himself.

Their date was seven o clock that night, he had started to get ready from four that evening, he had a haircut, shave and manicure his nails, pedicure his feet, had a luxurious bath with different aromatheraphy foam bath, brushed his teeth and put on a new suit, he bought from Harrods, he was nervous like a schoolboy going on his first date, the log bath calmed him down a lot.

He put on an expensive aftershave and was looking elegant and distinguished in his suit, he had arranged for them to have dinner in the air in his aircraft and also in Newyork at the Trump towers

All this surprise awaits her and she not even aware of what was happening he arranged with her personal assistant who got her passport from her house and he got the visa's without her even knowing about it, there was an overnight bag packed already for her.

Yvonne thought they were going for dinner somewhere nice in the west end, she did not know she will dine twice, in the air and Trump Tower, Yvonne was taking her time with her appearance to look good that afternoon, she visited her hairdresser who told her she was due for a facial after fixing her hair, she looked a million dollars with her new contact lenses that makes her eyes look brown bright and sexy, Yvonne was wearing a black dress that showed off her nice figure and long legs, she was attractive with her short hair cut in a bob and her well manicured fingers painted in deep red to go with her lipstick,

She looked great and was all set to go clutching her small evening purse, she put off the light in her bedroom as she waited in the living room for Ralph to pick her up, she walked elegantly to the door

Opened the door and was shocked to see Ralph looking twenty years younger dressed smartly and was looking very cool, she gave him a peck on the cheek she invited him in, she complimented him on his appearance and he said thank you, he told her she was looking very good herself.

They went outside to a limousine waiting for them, the chauffer came out and opened the door for them and they got in, Wow Yvonne said this is great, Yvonne checked out everything in the limousine Ralph brought out a bottle of champagne and opened it they toasted to each and Yvonne was like a child tasting her first lolly in a candy shop.

Where are we going for dinner she asked Ralph, he refused to tell her, its a surprise he quipped, honey please be patient and enjoy the ride, Yvonne did not ask any questions again as they drove all the way to a private airfield and boarded a private jet, she asked him where they were going to as he was beginning to scare her.

He said she should not be scared as he was not kidnapping her she should trust him, she said she trusted him , they got on the jet with Yvonne open mouthed and was really shocked about everything, no one had dined her in this style before it was a scene out of Hollywood she was really dumbfounded but try to relax like she does it all the time but she still could not relax.

She started to cry because everything seem so unreal to her, he calmed her down and kissed her gently and stroked her hair in a very tender way, he asked for dinner to be served with more champagne, they were served by two chefs, they received Vip treatment all the way and she enjoyed herself all the way even dancing with Ralph at a point.

They arrived at JFK airport and Yvonne was laughing and screaming, very excited and happy and kissing Ralph, thanking him for all the good time he had given her tonight, what she did not know was that more fun awaits her, and he had got her where he wanted her, she is sucked in now he knows she will not be able to resist him now.

# Chapter 8

The sun was going down and it was getting dark, everyone was gone from the beach except for Annabel who was walking along the beach crying as she was lost and could not find Phillips, they were together twenty minutes ago before she went to get Jamaica Pattie for them and when she came back he had disappeared, she went to the hotel room and waited for two hours, she did not find him and went back to search for him, did not find him she wanted to call the cops then she thought he was a big boy who can handle himself, then it hit her like a bolt of lightening that he might have gone off with another woman.

Annabel did not think she could be so stupid and carry on the way she did when she knew his reputation, she break down and cried, as it was cruel blow for him to behave so appalling to her like this right under her nose after paying for this expensive holiday and leaving her job and kids at a moment notice she must be really mad she thought, she took her bag and went to the hotel room to sit and wait for him, she waited the whole night and slept in her clothes on the chair.

He walked in at twenty past ten in the morning and saw her sleeping on the chair, he woke her up and she was startled and jump as soon as she realised it was him she started to punch him with clenched fist and he begged her that he was sorry and won't do it again, he went on about being hungry and if he should order breakfast or if they should go downstairs to eat.

Annabel was dumbfounded and very angry, she did not know what to say or do, she told him to do whatever he wanted, she threw his bag out of the door and warned him she never wanted to set eyes on him again as he disgust her, fine he said, he gathered all his stuff and ran out of the room to the tv presenter that he just met, he thought he had nothing to lose, as he was bored anyway with Annabel, the new lady was much prettier and rich.

Annabel knew his reputation but she thought he would have waited till they got back at least before getting another lover, he was a real dog, but she was not going to waste her holiday she was going to enjoy herself, she made her way to the reggae night concert that was held that night in another island, she dressed provocatively in a low short dress that was clinging to her body, as soon as she got there heads were turned in her direction she looked around the crowd and saw a guy sitting by himself smoking and drink in his hand watching her.

She went to the bar bought a drink and was chatting to him all night, his aloofness and sense of intrigueness seem to fascinate her, he was charming interesting and she was looking for some company tonight, it was an interesting night making love over and over again.

He showed her the rest of the island, they were together most of the holiday together they made love under the stars at night and swam afterwards, it was the most romantic man she had ever met

She knew the meaning of the word that says every disappointment is a blessing, when she compared Donald to Phillip he was just a boy, and Donald treated her with respect she knew it was not a wasted trip, he wanted her to extend her holiday so they could spend more time together she said she could not as there was too much at stake, her children and her business.

He told her he understood perfectly and will come and visit her in England, the departure at the airport was weepy and she felt like she was loosing a good man that she will never see again, but she got hold of her emotions, she kissed him really hard and off she went to board the aircraft to England,

 As she sat down in the aircraft to relive her fond memories of the romantic holiday she had afterwards, behind her she heard a laugh and she turned to look, it was Phillips and another female ogling and kissing each other, she did not feel anything for him, not even a pang of jealousy like she felt before, all she felt was sorry for his new conquest because he was going to find another person and dump her once he was bored and finish spending her money.

The aircraft took off in ten minutes at midnight to arrive at heathrow airport the next morning, she slept in peace and dreamed about Donald the whole night that he came to visit her in England and they were living together , the air stewardess woke her up by announcing that they had arrived and the aircraft was going to disembark and they will be joining the shuttle buses soon.

They disembarked and waited in queues at the arrival hall and soon they were out of the hall, Annabel hailed a black cab and told the driver where to head to and she was looking forward to see her kids that she had not seen in two weeks.

# Chapter 9

Rebecca wrote her book out of curiosity, she saw the advert seeking budding writers to apply by sending their manuscripts, it was staring her in the face at the bus stop, she looked at it for a long time and decided she will give it a shot, she thought if it goes well it was her ticket to breaking away from the band as she was becoming too obsessed about killing Natasha.

She knew if she did not leave she was going to strangle her very soon the writing will be the perfect way she thought, Rebecca took two months to write the manuscript about murdering her mother and other experiences in her life, she did not say it was a true story she called it fiction, the story was gripping ,tantalising and interesting, as soon as it was published it went to best sellers list because it sounded more real life, after so many book sales it was made into a hard cover and a film.

She started to earn big bucks, she break the news to Natasha that she was leaving them and will like to concentrate more on her writing now.

She was doing very well now, she is happy that she is more in control of her destiny now, she did not say anything to any of the girls until the book was published and was in the bookshops, that was when she told them which shocked Natasha as she thought they were friends that shares so much secrets together, she told her she will not be able to work with them again as she had a lot of book

Signing meetings come soon, Natasha could not put her finger on it but she knew Rebecca does not want to be friends with her again but just being civil, anytime she was in the same room as her she feels weird chills run down her spine, she could sense jealousy and rivalry going on in the room in a quiet subtle way but she could not explain the chills she could sense fear and knew that she Natasha will have to be avoiding Rebecca from now on, come to think of it she does not know much about this girl. She also noticed that she was very happy with other people except her.

She asked Natasha if she could leave immediately and she said yes that it was fine, Rebecca left and was over the moon that she did not have to kill anybody or play second fiddle to anyone again.

Rebecca seed of jealousy was building up again when she thought about all the millions that Natasha

Had made, even though she had left the band, and was making money herself now she thought it will be easy to get rid of her she planned and schemed the whole time that she would disappear into thin air without a trace, she discredited and assassinated her behind her back by leaking stories to the press who paid her millions and serialised the story for a week she made up all kinds of lies and make them swear not to reveal where the source of the informations came from, she also paid people who came forward with different stories to tell the tabloids.

She goes to Natasha place to stay with her for days to comfort her and get more information each time she was with her.

Throughout her ordeal Natasha was very sad, she searched her mind and try to figure out where this vendetta to get rid of her was coming from, but she could not figure out it was Rebecca, as she had gone to be her usual self and at the moment was very caring and nice, she even felt guilty in suspecting her because she thought she might be having problems hence the strange behaviours, she quickly drop her guard and was all nice to Rebecca even suggested they do lunch together as she was not going to the studio that afternoon.

Rebecca agreed and went along to Natasha's house that evening at eight, she had bought a hatch back Mercedes sports car with a new house she invited her to come and see the place, her humble abode, the house was tastefully furnished, it was very nice and comfortable, she was jealous of the house again as the humble abode was worth ten million pounds, the antiquities and ethnic decorations were from Asia.

Rebecca who did not have any taste in house decorations does not bother to decorate herself, she employed interior designers to design her home, but seeing what Natasha had done she knew she had good taste she mixed old and new with lots of ethnic mixtures which blends the neutral colours

She knew she was drab and had no class, that seems to infuriates her the more, Natasha could dress her figure perfectly with dress and it would fit, when they were in the band she would work out all the time but she was not bothered with the workouts, she was only doing it because the rest of the girls were working out as well, she loves junk food a lot and was not bothered about her weight, Rebecca has big bones so was always on the big side, so she was always pressured to loose weight by the band manager who was sometimes appalled by the things she eat.

All that contributed to her hating Natasha because she did not have that kind of non chalant attitude

That she had, Natasha was dedicated to the band, watches what she eat, and exercise a lot, even when they had finishes with a tedious concert.

They climbed into the car and zoomed off into the fresh summer night, the breeze blowing in their hair and face, with lavender smelling in the air around the surrounding garden, she was playing Marvin gay song and it was blasting away, Natasha was chatting animatedly to Rebecca but she was taking it all wrong like Natasha was showing off and she was not, that's how she had spoken to her

From the beginning , do you have a boyfriend now she asked Rebecca playfully, no she replied and was really mad at Natasha thinking maybe she should just strangle her now, but she refrained from doing it as she thought she has to plan it and execute it properly.

# Chapter 10

Douglas waited in his car with a cigarette in his mouth outside of the empire building he watched people walking up and down the road, the traffic was building up rapidly, he watched the couples kissing and cuddling each other in a tight embrace as they waited to take the lift to his favourite spot where a lot of this couple's had proposed to each other, he could see love in their eyes as they gazed happily into each others eyes, they were happy and contended with life, he became jealous because he had not known love all his life.

All Douglas had known was work and nothing else, he was a workaholic, he was thirty seven years and never had a steady girlfriend he was never home for a week, he had travelled all over the world clinging deals all over the place, relationships were hard to form for him as he was always a part time lover he was not always there.

Douglas realised he will never marry if he did not slow down, he told himself he was going to retire at forty and settle down to have kids because his parents are worried about him, they are yearning to have grand children.

Douglas had slept with high class whores in every city that he had been it was beginning to depress him as he wants to have a nice relationship with a normal girl that will chat with him and they could love each other, his condom burst several time so he had to go have a check in the hospital, and the test came back negative, it really scared him to think that he would have caught something in just a matter of minutes.

He saw some guys walking around the place he was packed and he asked them what the problem was, they said it was none of his business as it was a free country, they could walk about anywhere

They felt like going, he was shocked at their aggression and he explained that he will like to have a word with them, they said they were not ready to talk to him, so he beckoned to them to wait and listen to him, they were being rude to him because they thought he was English, as he spoke in America accent, they stopped to listen to him, he told them he lived in England but was here on business, and he could help them, as soon as they heard that they were ready to listen to him and he explained that he was not trying to pick them up or anything he is straight but he just wants to help them put something back to the community, give somebody a break, they were all ears to listen now.

He gave them his card and asked them to check on him the next day at his hotel, he was not aware that they were even homeless, they went to the shack that they were living got some clothes and went to a homeless shelter to have shower and get into decent clothes.

When they came to see him they were all looking very nice and he told them so, he asked them to dressing decent from today as people take you serious if you are neat and looking well, rather than looking scruffy and horrible.

He knew he was taking a big risk by allowing three men that he did not know to get close to him as he wants to help them and bring them to England to help change their perspective about life so they could see another part of the world and work harder to succeed in life.

He asked them to get their passports, and visa so that they should come to him and he will give them spending money and the tickets, they came to him as they promised as they were keen themselves.

They were really keen, they brought all their families all the way from Minnesota to see him and told them they will be going to college there, the families were excited.

Douglas met the lads for dinner with the rest of his family who wanted to meet the benefactor, they sat round the table, laughter ringing loud, everybody trying to speak at the same time with excitement, laughter and questions trying to ask him why he was helping them total strangers, he looked at them and told them his story, how he was struggling when he was a child and he promised to help somebody if things get better for him, they now understood where he was coming from, they thanked him and left.

Douglas was deep in thought, he knew he did the right thing helping this lads with scholarship, but he wondered and questioned himself if he will ever be happy and settle down with a wife and kids.

Three years later

Yvonne married her man, had a grand fairy tale wedding and living at the lap of luxury with a successful business.

Rebecca became a successful writes sold millions of books but never satisfied with anything in life, still very bitter evil, envious and manipulative as ever still planning to kill her friend some day.

The end.

# About the Author

Eunice is Nigeria born and has been writing for a long time. She schooled in England. At the moment Eunice is reflecting all the realities of life in her book to enable readers to appreciate the characters portrayed.